Lunar series book two :

# False

# Trails

## 2nd Edition

## By Whittney Corum

False Trails 2

Cover by vikncharlie

Whittney Corum

# Prologue

*A roar filled the air as blood was seeping into the ground. All eyes turned from the scarlet pool we made to the sky. Our eyes watched as our death sentence was ready to take place.*

*I watched as others tried to run, only to feel the heat of anger. I watched as their ash blew against the mighty wind that came from the wings above us. I watched as others readied their arrows tipped with the blood of another kill before this.*

*Our elfin archer readied his bow as my eyes went to the dragon. I then whispered a simple spell that I knew from heart. The spell brings focus only on myself. A spell that could bind a dragon, even a dragon who was 500 years old.*

*I then heard the whistle of the arrow and watched as it made it home in the dragon's chest. I then watched as the dragon fell to the ground. I saw others were ready to attack the dragon.*

*I then heard the voice of our Master telling them to hold back. I felt his eyes on me, and I nodded. I was always the one to see if the dragon was still alive. It was because they believed that I was the best choice since I had no family.*

*I walked over to the dragon, not surprised that he was still breathing. I got out my sword and -readied myself to end it. Yet when I was close enough, the dragon looked me dead in the eye.*

*"You killed my flare...and our soon-to-be fledgling..."*

*"She tried to warn you..." I replied, my grip tightening around my sword.*

*"You would punish her for the same love that yer own mother..."*

*"Enough," I growled as I sliced the neck of the dragon.*

*"Traitor..." was the last word that I heard.*

*"Yes, I am."*

*Though I do not know who I betrayed, my human friends or the dragon who raised me.*

## Anwil

The cobblestone streets of Mer were full as I walked through. I was here to buy supplies for another hunt. I was also told by my master that I would have to find another healer.

I sighed. Our last healer had died during our hunt, and I knew that most new healers wouldn't last long with our group. It was either because they were killed or, when finding out what we were hunting, would quit.

My eyes scanned the stalls of the market. Mer was the trade city for the land of Kardain. It was also the capital of the slave trade, a trade that most people believed was normal in Mer, but in the kingdom of Zodiac, only a week ride from here it was unpopular to own a slave.

I shook my head. My hand went to my neck, fingers touching my slave's mark as I looked to the west. A month's ride would lead to the Diana mountains and The Brother's pass. The home for clans of Finis, Maccons, and the loathed Slithers.

If one took the pass they would find a path which dived. One way would take someone to the Bone Cliffs, about a  two month journey; while the other path would lead a person to the Elfin high city of Rinbow. It would take a person three month's to ride to the city, if they could even get past the gates which protected it.

I knew all of this because of my friends who had been slaves, like myself. A full-blooded elf named, Badar, and a shifter of the Maccons clan, a man named Freki. They were elders who had taken a liking to me and had taken me under their wing when I was five summers old.

I shook my head and went back to the task at hand. I need to get the supplies and find a healer. Over the noise of the crowd I heard a loud voice filled the air. It was a call for an auction, and I found myself walking towards it.

It didn't take me long to see the wooden stage where the captured, elves, shifters and humans stood. I scanned the lineup until my eyes caught a figure behind the rest. I found myself staring at the figure was grabbed by a slaver and brought forward.

"Here's a treat, an elfin and shifter cross. Found outside the area of snakes."

The cross had spun gold hair with hints of white. Her skin was pale, and her eyes were as blue as jewels. I could tell she both angry and afraid of the situation she was in. I looked at the crowd around me and saw that others were coveting her just as I was.

I shivered, knowing that if the girl was bought by the men giving her that look she would be used to warm their beds.

"She is a healer."

That got my attention, and that of the others. A slave that was also a healer would be useful for anyone. As a slave they would be forced to do any healing that their masters wanted. For my master it would be cheaper, and the healer wouldn't stop healing when they found out what we were doing.

"Starting bid is 10 gold."

I waited, I needed to time my bid right. My eyes looking at the girl again, who was biting her lip. I then heard the bid reach the amount of 30 gold pieces. I took a breath.

"50 gold pieces."

Everyone looked at me, and once they realized who I was and who I belong too they backed off. I watched as the seller saw me too and nodded as he heard no more bids. He then shouted out for the whole crowed to hear.

"Sold, 50 gold pieces to the servant of Lord Gael."

I went over to the seller's desk and put the 50 gold pieces down. Then took the rope that held the girl's hands together. After paying I pulled the rope and led her to my master's house.

I had already bought the supplies and sent them ahead to the house. This left me with time to talk with the new servant that my master would have. We walked only a few blocks when the girl started to talk.

"Where are we going?" her voice was scratchy.

"To the house of my master, your new home."

"No, I need to go..."

"Sorry but you can't, you've been bought by Lord Gael."

"No, I was bought by you..."

"I'm one of the slaves to Gael."

"Slave..."

"Yes, now please save your voice. I'll get you water once were in the house."

I was glad when the girl decided to listen. She would make a great slave in our house. Unlike most, Gael treated his slaves like they were people instead of livestock.

I felt my body relax when we went through the gate. I was immediately attacked by a gray wolf. I had to laugh a little, and then the wolf turned his attention to the new slave.

"Yes, she's a shifter and elf cross, and our new healer."

I then watched as the wolf transformed into a middle-aged man. Freki was about a head taller than me which meant that he was twice as tall as the new slave. His hair was brown but with hints of silver. His eyes were a soft gold color and his tanned skin was covered with scars.

"What's yer name, and who's yer sire?"

"My name is Ingrid, daughter of Bran head of the Clan of Finnis." the girl replied.

"I heard that Bran had two daughters, you are the younger."

"Yes, and who are you?"

"Freki the first son of second son of Lupa the head of the Maccons."

"A gray wolf…but why..."

"Youth was hard on me, and I was foolish, and what about you pup?"

"I was trying to hire a team to kill a dragon."

"Then you found them but not the way that you wanted."

"What do you mean..."

"Anwil, who is this?" I heard the voice of my master.

## Ingrid

I turned my head to the voice I heard. Standing before me was a human who was about twenty summers old. His hair was a dark brown and his eyes were a hazel color. He wore robes that showed his status as a lord, or at least a human lord. The cloth was a dark green and gold.

"This is a healer, a bought slave." I heard the boy, Anwil replied.

"I can see that, now release her."

I looked closer at Anwil as he cut my ropes. He had black curly hair which was cut close to his scalp. His skin was tanned, and his hands weathered from work. Yet, when I looked into his eyes, I saw that they had a deep golden hue.

After my bonds were cut the man, Lord Gael was what the hunter had called him when I was bought, , motioned for me to come to him, I growled and crossed my arms, staying where I was. I was on a mission to find my sister and kill the dragon who forced her into a marriage. I was not here to be ordered around.

To my surprise he smiled and moved toward me. I then felt a magic spell wrapping around me. It made me loosen my arms and stand up straight. I hate controlling magic, and this magic made me feel like a mare ready to be bought.

"Easy, I don't want to hurt you. I want to look at you."

"Yeah, I know what you want to look at." I hissed.

"You do have a spirit, although you're a bit too young for me." he replied.

"I have you know I'm 16 summers old."

"Yes, and still a child for human kind."
"I'm not a human."

"Yet, you are still a child."

I huffed. Even by both elf and shifter standards I was still a child. Even so, I was old enough to exact revenge on the dragon who took everything from me. I was going to save my sister and bring my family back together.

"That may be, but I have a mission."

"Oh? Is that why you are out of your clan's land."

"Yes, and how would you know?"

"About shifter clans? I have been studying them for a long time. Elves too."

"Why?" I found myself asking.

"That's my mission, but now I would like you to come with me. We need to talk about your contract."

"Contract?"

"It's like an oath, only on paper."

I then felt the magic holding me break. I watched as he took a few steps, turning his back to me. I had the chance to flee to the gate, but something told me that I would be stopped before I even took two steps. I might not be hunter like my papa and sister, but I was no fool. So, I took a breath and followed the man who had bought me.

I followed him into the house, where the magic I felt a few moments ago seemed to be stronger. I held the fabric of my dress as we entered a room that I appeared to be his study. My eyes widened seeing the amount of books that lined the walls of the room.

There was a fire place between the book shelves and hanging on the wall over the mantle was painting of knight attacking a dragon. I was entranced by it, the colors and depth of it made me feel that I was immersed in the scene.

"It's a painting of my grandfather. He killed the dragon who kidnapped a lord's daughter."

"Dragons...they are menace."

He raised an eyebrow, turning to me, "You sound like you know of their deeds."

"A dragon put my sister under a spell and killed my papa." I replied turning to him.

"Then you will fit well here."

"Here?"

"Come. I want you show something."

I nodded as I watched him walk to the table in the middle of the room. It was so large that it took up most of the floor. On top of the table was a large map of Kardain, that had the elfin lands and shifter territories marked.

"I didn't know there was a human map that had..."
"My grandfather made it when he was traveling and marked where he had allies that could tell him about the activity of dragons."

"And these red X's on the map?"

"Where my group has killed dragons."

"You kill dragons?" I gasped in shock. I had been bought by the man who I came here to find. A man who would kill dragons. The goddess had blessed me in my search. "So, you'll help me?"

"Well, most people would say that because you serve me, you'll help me. Tell me about this dragon who took your sister."

I took a breath and started to tell my new master about what had happened to my family. For the first time in a long time I felt hope that I had finally found a way to get my sister back from the dragon who took her from me.

## Damion

The high council was composed of the children of the first dragon and his loyal knights. They hailed from all over world, yet they all come here to Dragos Peak, otherwise known to the world below as Teris mountain.

I, a southern shifter, was here because I was a messenger to the Queen of Dragons. She was currently resting in one of the caves with her son, the heir of dragons. I was here to tell her about what went on when she wasn't here. The things her husband would try to hide from her.

It wasn't that the king didn't love his queen, he hid things because he worried about how my lady would react to the news. I couldn't help but agree with him, especially now since it was close to the time that the queen would give birth to a pup.

"Greetings, my brothers: Alik, the breath of wind from the north, Roka the sage of water."

Alik was a pure white dragon with light blue scales on his belly and chin. He was one of the larger dragons in the meeting. Roka was one the smaller dragons, and had dark blue scales with a beard and an underbelly of white.

"And my sisters: Elektra the fire of the south, Kaya the blossom of the west."

Elektra was a dragon who was bright red with sunset color scales around her eyes, wings, and belly. She was as tall as Alik but unlike him she wore a frown.

Then my eyes went to the smallest of the assembled group. Kaya seemed to be younger than the rest of the dragons. Her scales were a dark brown, almost the color of soil, while her belly scales were a dark green. Yet around her body and eyes there were splashes of color shaped as flowers.

Blagdon, the King of Dragons, was the largest of them all. His scales were a mixture of dark green and black, while his underbelly scales were a deep purple. His mismatched eyes of green and black were staring at the dragons before him.

"I thank you, lord of all dragons." I heard the humming tune of Roka's say.

"As do I," Alik followed.

"I speak for both the south and west. Thank you for this audience." Elektra spoke.

"Now on to our reason for this meeting."

"There have been murders of dragons, all here in Kardain, and some on the borders of Sollin."

Sollin, was a small country to the south of Kardain. I knew of it because my own home, Helios, was a few months of travel by boat. I had been to Sollin before and what stuck out in my mind was the warlord that ruled there. He kept his land guarded, so whoever was hunting dragons either was very foolish or had ties to Sollin.

"Yes. At the last count we have lost eight dragons, most of them from the south but they seemed to shifting west." Blagdon was looking at Kaya.

"I have lost three dragons...and there has been a development."

"What do you mean?"

"The last dragon who was killed...he was brought into a rage. His flera was killed, along with the fledgling that she was carrying."

"Who was it?" Alik growled.

"Titus..."

The room began to freeze. I was tempted to transform into my animal and was about to but then the voice of Blagdon filled the air.

"Calm yourself, Alik."

"Titus was one of the elder dragons, he was there when your grandfather became king." Alik growled.

"As you were, and I knew him too. That doesn't mean we lose our heads."

"Are you saying that because you believe it, or are you thinking about your wife's sister who wants you dead." Alik spat angrily at his father.

"My flera isn't the reason..."
"Don't play us for fools, we all know the rumors about your flera's sister seeking revenge."

"Alik, you are close to be dismissed." Blagdon warned.

"And you're letting your feelings for your flera cloud your judgement."

I felt a cold gaze directed at me. I answered it with a smirk, I wasn't going to be shaken by an old dragon. I was the son of a clan leader. I was taught to stand up for myself.

"You even let those who aren't dragon to come into meetings." Alik sneered

"Damion is here because my queen wishes it."

"I still-"

"Enough Brother Alik," Kaya interrupted, "I have to agree with our king. Even if his sister-in-law is part of the murder pack, that doesn't mean his queen is part of them," she reasoned with the elder dragon.

"Only a novice dragon would say that."

"This novice is one of the council." Blagdon said as he stood up.

I watched as the ice dragon sighed and turned his back to the council. He then spoke to everyone in the room.

"I will say nothing else, but if any of my blood or dragons from my land are killed. I will not be hesitant to kill every hunter I find. Even if the hunter is the sister of queen of dragons."

Now I needed to leave. I need to tell milady what happened. I ran to the small cave where milady and her son were waiting. I hoped that when I arrived milady would be in a good mood.

...

Astrid, adoptive daughter of Bran, head of the Clan of Finnis, the true child of Flickron the God of Tricksters and the Lady of Lace, also known as the Queen of Dragons was waiting for me. As I walked in she was playing with her adopted son, her snow white hair and pale skin shining as she turned a pair of gray sky eyes to look at me

"Milady, I have news..."

"Damion, ye don't do have to talk like that."

I relaxed. It seemed that she was in a good mood. She had been switching between moods for a few months. Though there was a good reason for it, it still made me shake when she was angry. I smiled at her, "How are you feeling?"

"I'm 7 months along with a pup, I can control my feelings."

I blinked; she could control her mood swings? This was the first time that I heard she could, though it might be because she was close to her due date. I shook my head and sat on the bed beside the prince of dragons and adopted son of Astrid.

"Uncle Damion!"

"Hey, Aiden. How's your duty watching your mother?"

"Good."

I smiled at the small dragon. I had grown attached to the little one, ever since I began work with the dragons and milady. I then turned back to milady who was staring at me, her hands on her belly.

"So?"

"The murders have increased, and Alik thinks your sister is to blame."

"Of course. It makes sense, but we don't know if she joined a group yet..."

"My allies last saw her on the road to the human city of Mer."

"That was three weeks ago, and the mirror lost track of her."

The mirror was a gift from Astrid's aunt Solara, goddess of the sun. It was mirror that would show the wielder what they wanted to see. It also showed the true image of a person or creature. It was helpful to us to watch the movements of Astrid's sister, but now it seemed it was broken or that someone was blocking the image.

"Yes, and I'm afraid that Alik is going to kill your sister on sight," I warned her

"Really..."

I watched as she gripped the table close to her. I could see it shake from her grip. I took a breath and stood up.

"Astrid, you need to calm down."

"I am..."

"Your grip is breaking the table."

"Oh..."

A deep voice in the doorway startled both of us, "Listen to your messenger, my queen."

We both turn to see Blagdon and Roka. I bowed my head knowing that I should leave. It was time for Astrid to have a checkup for the babe that she carried, and Roka was the doctor of the queen. I hope that I would be able to give good news to milady soon.

## Anwil

I was putting the goods I bought into the storage house when a voice spoke behind me.

"So, you bought a daughter of Elfin blood."

"Nice to see you too Badar." I replied turning around.

Badar's face was set in a frown, which wasn't unusual. He was an elf who showed his love, worry, and all other emotions with a frown. I was used to it, because I knew that under that frown his eyes told his true emotion.

"Yes, her name is Ingrid..."

"I know that name, she's the daughter of Maira, one of the granddaughters of the High King."

"Yet, she was sold as a common elf," I replied watching his frown get bigger.

"A common elf is still higher than a human..."

"In whose eyes Badar?"

We both turned around to see our master, along with Ingrid, walking toward us. It seemed that in the time between meeting with our master and coming here, she had been to the servant baths and given new dress. Her hair was loose, framing her face and hanging down her back. It was a melted gold color and her lavender eyes bore straight into me.

"I mean no disrespect." Badar stated, interrupting my thoughts on Ingrid.

"I know, some believe that elves are higher than humans, yet when one goes into the slave markets, one finds that all beings are close to the same price, rather it be an elfin prince, or a peasant's son."

Badar bowed, as our master turned to me. I bowed and then stood up. I couldn't help but smile seeing the gentle smile of my master. He then looked at Ingrid who blushed a little.

"Anwil, I want you to show Ingrid where she'll be living. Also, we need to get ready for a new hunt."

"Of course, and when will we be leaving master?"

"In one week, I want all the stores counted before we leave."

I humbly nodded as our master left, taking Badar with him. I knew the two would be talking about the trip ahead. They usually did this, and that would mean that Badar and our master would be eating late into the night.

"They are close?"

I looked at the elfin-shifter beside me and nodded.

"Master and Badar grew up together, before Badar was taken hostage and bought by master's father."

"Oh..."

"But if they're friends..."

"Why didn't he release Badar when he inherited the land?

"Badar's family was murdered a few years into his slavery. He has nothing to go back too."

I watched as she bit her lip and hugged herself. I resisted the urge to comfort her, as I was a man and she was a young girl in every society that I had learned about. I took a breath and looked at her.

"We must get you to your room."

"Right..."

I simply nodded, I did not want to cause her anymore pain or bad memories. I started walking into the servant's house and opened the door. We were walking down the main hallway when she started to speak again.

"This is a slave house?"

"We call it the servant house now; our master keeps us as slaves only by name."

"Then you can leave at any time?"

"When our master wishes or when we are killed."

"Killed?" I heard her asked shaking a little.

"We hunt dragons, death is a real risk."

"I know that but..."

"You are a child."

I watched as she pouted, and I sighed. I wanted her to understand how much was at stake when fighting with dragons. The price that many a friend has had to pay for the rest of us to survive.

We stopped at a door that I knew all too well. I had shown the room to about twenty healers before her. I opened the door and watched as Ingrid walked in.

"I'll leave you to get settled. Dinner is at sundown."

"Okay." I heard her answer.

I just shook my head and went to my own work. I wanted to make this hunt safe for all of us. It was my duty as decoy for all hunts.

Whittney Corum

## Ingrid

I watched as the boy left, leaving me alone in the small room which I would call my own now. I looked around the new room, it was set up for a healer alright. The room had a wooden table with a bound volume of healing. I walked over to it, my footfalls seemed to echo on the stone floor.

The volume was well kept, only a small amount of dust was on it. I dusted it off to see a mark of human healer. A great tree which reached both the sky and earth, and a beautiful wren on the tree. So, the owner of the book was a servant and believer in Faia.

I was not surprised, the elfin healers I had met told me that the best human healers believed that the youngest goddess was a beauty with the power over nature. I could believe that most of elfin healers were taught to respect other healing practices and god or goddess who use them. I shook my head; I went away from my teacher and became an avenger to save my sister.

I used my magic to see if there was a magic spell on the volume in my hands. It was only a simple protection spell. I undid it and then opened the volume. I found that it wasn't a book on potions and spells for healing but also the personal thoughts of the healer who owned the volume.

I found myself sitting down on the bed across the room. The volume was once owned by Mercy Hanna, a human from a small village outside the human kingdom of Zodiac. She came here when she got a letter from her cousin who worked in town. She found employment with this house and lived here in this room for about three months.

I stopped from reading more because of the chimes playing. It was a call to dinner, and my belly needed some protein. I got up and laid the volume on the bed, marking my place so when I got back, I would read more about the woman I had taken the place of.

☐

I was surprised that when servants of the house went to dinner they didn't eat in the kitchen. We were led to the main hall to eat with Lord Gael. If I hadn't known any better, I would have thought that everyone was a group of friends sitting for a meal. The only thing that stopped the scene from being that was the marks on some of the older slaves' necks.

"Tonight, we rejoice to have our new healer, Ingrid join us for the next hunt."

"Welcome." I heard the voices of the men around me.

"I should introduce you to our group." Gael stated as the men nodded.

"The elf to the left of me is Badar, he belonged to my father, and is now my dearest servant. To my left is a person you already know, Anwil. Then there's Freki, he's the wild coin in our purse."

I nodded and stood up introducing myself to the men.

"I'm Ingrid, the daughter of Bran, head of the Clan of Finnis. I'm also the youngest daughter of Maira, the granddaughter of the High King of Elves." I replied feeling proud as I said it.

"Welcome Ingrid to our little band." Gael replied a soft smile on his lips.

"Thank you…"

"How did the daughter of Finnis find herself in the hands of slavers?" Freki asked.

I then took a breath and told them the story of how I had chosen to find my sister and save her from the dragon who put a spell on her. How on my journey I happened to be caught by hunters and was taken to the slave pens where I was sold and bought by Anwil.

"Aye, that's a good story, I do like your will also. I'll be happy to slay the dragon that has taken hold of yer sister."

Badar nodded in agreement while Anwil looked at his plate. Gael just smiled and then took a sip of his drink. I sat back down and started to eat my own meal. I didn't know why but these men seemed to make me feel at ease. I just didn't know how easily that could be broken.

### Damion

I hate going to midnight meetings. Not because of their mystery, no I can deal with that. It was having to change my sleeping patterns.

My meeting was in a little grove a few yards from the cave that housed the dragon and his family. I was standing by one of the taller trees when I heard footsteps. I looked to see the form of milady, covered in a hood of darkness.

"Milady, I didn't know you were the one who sent the note. So, are we going to run away together?" I joked.

"I'm loyal to my mate, I asked you to come here because I need a favor."

"My duty is to obey you, I do anything your order…"

"I want you to decide this yourself."

I nodded waiting for her question. It was one I knew she had been debating for a few weeks. Ever since we heard about the attacks on dragons.

"You want me to find your sister."

"How? Never mind, I guess I'm that easy to read."

"No, I know you love your sister as much as you love your mate, cub, and one that you carry."

"I would go myself, but as you know I can't."

"Yes, a seven-month cubbed maid traveling though the countryside would bring more questions than answers." I replied with a smirk.

"Yes, even though I have thought about it." she replied as she looked up to the sky.

"Of course you have, you are the daughter of the Trickster and he loves to rile things up."

This made my queen smile. She then placed her hand on her belly and sighed.

"The greatest gift in the world, is also my greatest weakness." She muttered.

"True, but it might also bring great joy. I mean, I know it's like to have younger siblings. It might not be like caring for your own child, but it's close enough."

"Your right, but I need you to act swiftly and carefully which is why I am giving you this."

I watched as she took off her cloak, her white, blond hair shining in the moon light like waves. She was embodiment of the Lady of Lace, at least that what I thought. Though it did help that her mother was the actual Lady of Lace.

"Milady?"

"Take the shift our lady made for my wedding, it will help you. I will check on your progress as much as I can."

"I'm honored to be at the center of your mind."

I smiled, watching her blush and then took a breath. I knew that milady was loyal to her mate but teasing her was too much fun. Even though I could be in hot water with her mate if I kept it up. I then looked around us. The scene to anyone else would be a couple meeting in the night.

"I must go before your guards think of us as lovers."

"Guards?" she raised her eyebrow.

"For a blessed child of a god and goddess you don't know much about protectors of the gods." I joked.

"Ya mean fairies?"

"They are the small elves that keep children safe right?"

"Not exactly…"

"I won't be much longer, I must leave. I promise though to write about my search."

"Hunt well, Damion."

"Be blessed milady." I replied taking her hand and kissing it.

With that I left the clearing, milady's shift transforming into a hood for myself. I felt a burning in my arm, knowing that it was time for a meeting with the other secret I had been keeping. The other reason I had come to the aid of milady, the secret that mother kept and would send my own kingdom to war.

## Anwil

I was called to my master's study during the night. It wasn't uncommon at least when we were getting ready to hunt. I walked in to see my master facing the fire his face close to it as he leaned in.

"Anwil, it's time to hunt again."

"Yes master..."

"Yet, this time is different from the last."

"Master?"

"Anwil, I was thinking after this I would release you all…"

"Master are you well?"

My master was kind, but I also knew most people in Mer would look down on him for setting free his slaves. Slaves were much like money and property the more someone had the richer they were in the eyes of people. So, I wondered why our master would let us go?

"This next hunt will be last, I want you all to be free no matter what happens."

"If you're sick I can see what our new healer can…"

"Ease Anwil, I'm just thinking ahead. I have received a letter from my mother's house. They wish that I marry."

"So you believe that your promised wife wouldn't support you in what you're doing?"

"She's of court, and would look down on slaves, while I think of them as equals. She would want us to live at court, not here…"

I nodded, I knew that my master would be worried about his promised wife. He was the only heir to his mother and father's house. It was his duty to have an heir, and to do that he needed to join his house with another. That would mean that his promised wife would be our mistress and my master didn't like that idea.

"Of what house is the lady from?"

"Gaia."

Gaia was one of famous houses here in Mar, and was the highest importer of slaves, especially those of human blood. I was taken by a distant cousin of that house and branded a slave because of it. I bit my lip and curled my fists, I knew it was childish, but it felt right to do it.

"Ease Anwil, that's why I will be setting all my servants free, I know how my promised wife's family acts towards slaves. I will make sure that all you are safely away before I marry."

"Even so, what about you master?"

"I will be fine, I can teach her my ways of thinking."

"Of course, master…"
"Thought it troubles me a little that the family would want a marriage now."
"Sir?"

"Sorry Anwil, I shouldn't worry you," he replied giving me a tried smile.

"Right sir."

"Now, back to job at hand."

"The hunt?"

"Yes, we're going to find a high lord of dragons. At least that is what I can tell from the description Ingrid told me."

"A high lord?"

"I don't know if it's one of the four council members, but I want to prepare just in case."

"What of his mate?"

"If we can convince her to come with us peacefully, we can allow her back..."

"And I will deal with the decision if she doesn't." I said standing up straighter.

"I can't ask you to do that."

"I already have blood on my hands, master."

"Dragons, not their mates, I hated that I have to use your power to down a dragon, I will not have the blood of their mates and families on your hands."

"Master…"

I watched as my master shook his head and then looked at the map again. I knew that the time for talking was over. It was time for duties.

"We know that when Ingrid's sister was taken it was in the Darin forest a few miles away from the brother's pass."

"A normal hunting ground for Finis clan…"

"Yes, I'm glad that my lessons in geography and Freki's history of shifters are taken root in you." My master said with a kind smile.

"Yes sir, but why would a shifter leave their group of three for hunting?"

"Ingrid's sister is eldest of her family, so what would take her away from her hunt?"

"A cry of a baby." I stated.

"That's what I thought, so the dragon who took her either transformed their voice or…"

"A hunter took a dragon babe and used it as bait." I replied noticing the frown on my master's face.

"Monsters, I know it sounds strange for me to say that. A dragon killer like myself hating hunters who take a babe dragon from its family."

"You are just master; you give a chance for the mate of the dragon to leave with their babe…"

He just nodded and then he pointed to a field that was a few leagues away from the forest.

"That would be big enough for a dragon to land, and it's far enough even on foot for a shifter-elfin cross to run."

"You think that's where the dragon found his babe and Ingrid's sister?"

"Yes, and by our other hunts his cave would be only a few leagues from it…"

"Unless the hunters took the babe from a nest far away and kept it away…."

"That's a good idea, but I don't think a hunter would risk that. They would use the babe as quick as they can to get their prey."

I nodded and scanned the area around or close to the field. By experience a dragon could fly about 300 miles before resting. So, the cave that the dragon called home had be between 2 to 3 days away from the field. It would be on a higher cliff face, because most of the dragons to the west were close to the wind and would stay in higher places.

"Anwil, don't forget the season." My master gently told me.

I nodded, sometimes if a dragon had a mate they would change where they lived. It was almost like the birds who fly south in the winter. I then glanced to the south, and my eyes caught the Agni's mountains, named because of their red color. It was the mountain range that between Kardain and Wilds, the forest known for the secretes and legends it owned.

My eyes caught the tallest of the mountains, Teris. It was tall enough for a sky dragon to live, and close enough to the Wilds that most humans wouldn't go near it. Also, the legend about it made it eerie also.

"Teris, the mountain of Magi." I heard my master breathed.

"It makes sense…many humans stay away because of the cult that used to live there." I replied.

"That was until they were all killed off because they killed one of Faia's blessed children."

I nodded. Out of the three goddesses, Faia was one of the most dangerous. Unlike her sisters who ruled over mortals, Faia oversaw all animals, and those humans who had a connection to the earth or animals. They're called her "children" and one of dearest was Teris, who was killed by the Magi in one of their rituals. So, the goddess turned them to stone or other animals had had them hunted and used to make weapons.

"Would dragons really live there?" I found myself asking.

"They would, since they would probably be those who are closest to Faia and most humans wouldn't travel there."

I nodded and took a breath. It was time for me to check our guess. I close my eyes and focus my power on the map. My mind was clear, and I started to see things.

...

*An elf-shifter woman was sitting in a grove near the high mountain. Beside her was a young boy with blond hair and green eyes. They were laughing, and I couldn't help but see that woman was with child.*

*The woman was singing a song to the boy who would help her. I couldn't help but think that the melody was something I knew from my past. I then heard footsteps and two men came into the field.*

*The boy ran to the younger of the men who had mix matched eyes and reddish black hair. He walked over to the woman and child giving them a soft smile. The other man walked to the woman and helped her up.*

*I could tell he was a healer from the east, yet he seemed much older than he looked. I could make out a few words that they were speaking.*

*"How are you feeling?" the healer asked.*

*"I'm fine...just worried."*

*The man nodded.*

*"It's normal for a new mother to worry."*

*"Even if she's the mate of the Dragon?" she asked with a small smile.*
*"Yes, and you doubly so because of him." the healer pointed to the other man.*
*"Hey, I'm not that bad." The other man replied holding the boy.*
*"Yes, you are." Both the woman and healer replied.*

...

I woke up and looked at my master. I couldn't believe it, the dragon that we would be facing wasn't a high dragon, he was the King of all Dragons. I knew that my master was right, this would be a different hunt. This hunt had only two ways of ending, the death of the King of Dragons or our own death.

## Ingrid

I was walking back to my room but I stopped when Balder blocked the door. The elf was older than my late mother and his golden hair with strips of white matched my own. He was frowning and I braced myself for a scolding. I was not ready though for him to take my hands and looked at them.

"These hands know about hard work, at least healing," he stated.

"I was a student in healing…"

"Yet, instead of taking the vows and learning from the elders of the elfin council, you decided that going after the grandchild of our king would be more useful than healing."

"If it means getting my sister back and having the rest of what of my family together, then yes." I replied stubbornly.

"I wonder if you're doing this for your sister or for your own selfish reasons?"

"Selfish, just because I want to save my sister?" I yelled at him.

I pulled my hands away and opened my door.

"Ask yourself this, does your sister needs to be saved?"

I slammed the door and growled. How dare he accuse me of being selfish? I, who gave up my own lessons to find and save my sister. Who wanted nothing more but to protect and keep my family together? I was still fuming when I looked at the volume on the table.

"I'm not a selfish…but…what if my sister loves the dragon…no, it's just a spell." I was fighting with myself, and I looked out the window and at the tree outside. I went over and touched one of the branches.

*"Green and brown a tree to be bound. Give me your power to heal and conceal scars on and around the feelings I bound."*

Whittney Corum

It was calming spell for healers, and it was one of the first we learn. It helped a healer to keep their thoughts focused on healing. All the healer need was a piece of green. This could be a tree branch, flower, or even moss, I used the tree because it was older and could hold more power.

I felt relieved that my thoughts were calmed and went to my cot. It was time for me to sleep and judging by the meeting tonight we would leave in the morning. I changed into my sleeping clothes and laid down. Closing my eyes to relax and found myself transported to my dreams.

☐

*The world is surrounded by darkness, the only way I could see is a light, though it is shadowed. I walked and then saw before me a scene which made my blood run cold. A mother and child running as a dragon stood behind them.*

*I froze watching as the two ran, my heart beating fast as I watched them being blocked by shadows. They turned and then saw the dragon fall, I thought they would be happy but I saw tears.*

*"Papa." The boy cried.*

*"Love…" the woman yelled.*

*I then watched as an arrow pierced her chest, as she fell she looked at her son. I watched as she called forth magic which took the boy away. Then a shadowy figure came into view, holding a sword. I found myself watching as the figure cursed not seeing the boy.*

*"He's out of reach now…" the mother stated.*

*"He'll be mine in time."*

*The scene turned into darkness again and I heard a voice in my ear.*

*"Protect the man, he'll save what's dear to you."*

*"Who said that?" I asked.*

*"Protect the man, He'll save what's dear to you."*
*Was my answer as darkness overwhelmed me, but I could*
*hear a voice calling out.*

*"Your sister is safe, but you are out of my reach."*

**Damion**

I made it to a small river as the pain in my arm
reached its height. I then put my arm in the river and began
the chant.

*"By the pain that I feel, show me the one that's*
*sealed."*

The water bubbled and twisted, turning black and
polluted until a bright red like blood filled it. The watered
cleared to show a woman dressed in black her eyes like
those of a snake and a smile which was both charming and
deceitful. Her eyes narrowed seeing the hood I wore.

"So, the blessed child gave her gift to you." Her voice sounds a hiss.

"Yes…"

"You're doing very well Damion, soon we'll be ready to rule this world."

"But remember your promise to me." I growled.

"Of course, no harm will come to your lady, the child she carries, or the little boy that you're so fond of."

"Good, I'm to find milady's sister."

"Yes, and my spies tell me that the girl will be with the one we need."

"I thought you said the boy was hidden from you?"

"Not when it's close to my celebration, soon Sollin will be ours."

"I will rule it well."

"And the moon will bless you for it, you will make the line pure again. But we first need the boy, the boy is only one that can stop us."

"I know…"

"I dealt with his mother and adoptive father, but he was protected. I need you to do this."

"Yes, Tanth."

The woman smiled as she raised her hand. I felt the warmth in my arm increase, and I had bite my lip so I wouldn't scream. I knew that she was enjoying it. She was mistress of pain and death in Sollin, Tanth the sealed spirit of vengeance and betrayal. The daughter of a fallen god and his mortal wife.

She was also my ancestor, the one raised who me when my mother and father were busy with other things. Her power held me and protected me all these years. She would give me the right to rule Sollin and I would give her the last of the line that sealed her away all those years ago.

"I'll leave it to you my sweet little boy."

With that the water switched back though it was still dark. I knew that it was poisoned and that anyone or anything that drunk from this small spring would become tainted with Tanth's magic. It was a fate of everything that I touched with my magic. I, who was once a hunter for the trickster now fighting to rule my own kingdom.

☐

A few hours later, I found a small inn. I opened the door to the smell of drunks and women. I walked to the bar keep who was fat man in his forties, and seemed to be cleaning an already spotless glass.

I sat at the bar and put two gold pieces down, one for a drink the other for information. I watched as the man pocketed both and gave me a glass of mead. I winced, but I guess he didn't have any wine.

"What can I do for you mister?" he asked.

"I want to know if there's anyone going on a hunt for dragons?" I asked taking a sip of the drink.

"You must mean Lord Gael, I heard that he going to hunt."

"Lord Gael?" I asked taking another sip of my drink.

"He's from a family that's known for killing dragons, I heard he was taking a break because of the loss of their healer. It seems that he's found a new one, so he's headed for a hunt."

"A new healer?"

"Yeah, a slave, an elfin shifter mix."

"More elf I take it?" I asked hiding my intent.

"Yep, and by all accounts a beauty, though she's a little young."

"Sixteen summers?"

"Why do you ask?"

"I'm looking for someone like that."

"Then good luck, my friend. Don't you know the price of stealing property from a lord?"

"No, but judging from your friends that have come closer as we've talk it's a pretty price."

"Very smart for a shifter." He replied as he motions to his friends for the kill.

I smirked as I side stepped one of them and blocked their attack. I then started to fight, my teeth sharping my claws coming out. These men wanted a fight, I would give to them. I could also feel magic pulsing through my veins. Tanth was wanting blood, and these fools are the ones who will feed my goddess.

Whittney Corum

## Anwil

I sighed as I checked everything again. We were getting ready to leave and my master

wanted everything to be ready. I was trying to push the vision I had last night out my head.

After I told our master who we were hunting, he said we must be ready for anything. I couldn't agree more. Our previous hunts had shown us that a dragon is more protective of their flera when she was expecting a child. So making sure we were ready was a must.

"Anwil, where's our healer?" I heard Balder asked.

"Don't worry, I'll fetch her." I replied, as I thought it would calm both myself and Balder down.

I walked into the servant's house to look for her. I saw that her door was open and I knocked on it. Thinking that she was asleep or in a different room, I went in. I did find her but only covered in a white towel and her hair wet.

"By the Lady of Lace…" she cursed as she saw me.

I felt myself turn red and I cast my eyes down. I figured that's why Balder chose me to find her. He must have known that she would be washing. I then heard the rustle of fabric, and the few curses that I thought I would hear from an elf.

"I am ..."

"Didn't your mother teach you do not barge into a woman's room without knocking?"

I frowned as my mother, a woman with brown hair and kind eyes, filled my mind. I pushed it away and sighed looking at the bags on the bed. They were only the size of a sack of wheat, but I could tell they were filled to the brim.

"Only two bags?"

"I was taught that sometimes it's better to travel light. Too many healing potions and books can weigh you down. Besides there are many plants in the wild that are used as healing herbs."

"I take it you know them..."

"As it was part of my test to start learning under a healer yes."

I simply nodded and looked at her. Her hair was now put up in a bun with bits hanging down, not to hide her sight, just because of the tie being lose. She wore a green hunters garb supplied by my master. I knew this because of the mark on the breast of the garb. Also, because it belonged to the last healer who left it here.

I found myself thinking about the last healer, who was homelier than the girl in front of me. Ingrid wasn't like Mercy, she was an elf and a child in both human and elfin years. She wasn't a woman who chose to come with us because I had asked her too.

Then I remembered the words that my master said last night, how he feared that this was a different hunt. I felt in myself for the first time in the years since the death of my mother and adoptive father the fear of killing a dragon. Feeling that it was something I couldn't do, or at least shouldn't try.

I shook my head, I was not the child afraid of power used by the dragon. I was Anwil loyal servant to the master who had saved me. The one who treated me kindly after the blood was shed in that cave. The cave where I had lived with the two people who I thought loved me.

"Are you ready then?" I asked walking to the door.

"Lead the way," she said as she followed me.

I prayed that this wouldn't be the same as the loss of Mercy.

## Ingrid

After the morning intrusion of Anwil, I was sitting on a small pony holding the reins of Freki's horse as he searched for game. We had been riding for a few hours and Lord Gael had decided that we needed to rest and suggested that the gray wolf hunt us some lunch. I was given the job of keeping track of his horse, which wouldn't have been so bad if I didn't have Balder staring a hole through me.

Yes, I knew that he thought that this trip, my mission was selfish, but I knew in my heart I was doing the right thing. I would save my sister and we would be happy living with my uncle. Maybe she'd find a nice elf or even a shifter to bond with, at least after the spell of the dragon wore off . A few looks from an elf who didn't support me didn't bother me.

☐

I was riding beside Freki while Anwil rode beside Lord Gael. Balder was to the left of the lord listening to them talk. I found myself gritting my teeth, I didn't know why but I felt jealous that I couldn't ride with them.

"Because yer a mix blood."

"What?"

"All mix bloods have that feeling, the feeling of bein' looked down upon because yer blood isn't that pure."

"I don't…"

"Because we're from the north, Balder there is from one of the southern holdings. He came from Magin."

"The place where female elves rule?"

"Yes, and where humans are treated like shifters and elves are treated here."

I nodded. I had heard mama talk about Magin, the place where her own father came from. She told me about how there, the elf who ruled was a female. She also told me that her father was related to the first queen of that land.

"My mother's father came from that land. The first queen's blood."

"So, you must have stronger elf blood than shifter."

"Yes. I always felt that I was more elf than my siblings."

The older shifter nodded as he helped me move along the small path that ran through the woods. I couldn't help but feel a little bit uneasy about the dark woods surrounding us. I guess everyone else felt the same way, because I felt our company draw closer together.

"Easy, little one."

"What's wrong with the forest?" I asked.

"So, ya do have some shifter blood."

"That didn't answer my question..."

"Hush, ye are feeling the voice of the wood. It's changed though, as if something dark has come though here."

"Dark?" I whispered.

"Yea…something that's not native…a blood lust that effects everything."

"In the woods?"

"No, to the land of Kardain."

I shivered at that; it was if as he spoke the words the darkness seemed to creep around us. I could feel my pony start to shake and paw at the ground. Freki's horse started to buck and neigh nervously. I then looked at the three in front of us and saw that their own horses were acting the same way.

"Steady everyone." I heard Gael say as the horses started to fight us.

"Ingrid, ya need to get off the pony." Freki's voice rang out.

I tried to obey but the pony started to panic and the next thing I knew it started to run. Tree branches scratched me like the claws of a wolf as we ran through the forest. I felt fear spread in my body as I realized I could no longer hear any of my party.

*Please don't let this be the end, I need to save my sister,* I prayed as I was taken deeper into the forest.

## Damion

I had been walking in the woods, the ruins of the inn burning behind me, when I was surprised to see a pony running toward me. I reached out to calm it and found that it did have a rider. An elf-shifter rider; a girl who couldn't be older than sixteen summers and was unconscious on the pony's back. Yet I couldn't help but smile at my luck.

"Lucky me, a horse and a girl." I mused as the mark of my arm glowed.

"Astrid…" I heard her say in a daze.

I raised any eyebrow. Could my mission be over this quick? The mission milady asked me to do? Then I felt pain in my arm. I winced and looked at down at it, remembering that my mission was only half done. I needed to find the boy now, and this one would lead me to him. It seemed that luck was truly on my side today.

☐

I followed the road and path that the horse came from. I noticed that it was close to the river where I had summoned Tanth. I could also feel her dark power stronger here, her seal was close to being open. Soon everything would be in place for her return to power. Yet I had to think about the task at hand.

I had gotten on the horse and propped her up before me. Her head was laying on my chest, her blonde hair tickling my neck. I was only a few feet from the road when I heard a growl. I looked to see a gray wolf, fur riddled with scars and his eyes glowing with a protective glare. I stopped the horse and eyed him. I could probably take him.

I then heard footsteps and saw that three more figures come out of the woods. One elf, one human, and one that I could not tell. This got my attention- there were few that could trick a shifter's nose. Even another shifter would have a distinct scent unless... I couldn't help but smile at my luck.

"Hello, it seems you have something that belongs to me. I would like her back." The human stated.

"You must be Lord Gael." I said with smile and bowed.

"Yes, and you are a shifter." He replied his hands were on his sword.

"How do you know that?"

"Because Freki caught your scent in the wind."

"Of course, a wolf shifter would catch my scent. so tell me what type of shifter am I?"

"Pridus." I looked to boy that said it his voice shaking a little.

"Correct, and you are?" I replied with a smile.

"Anwil is my friend and servant."

I held back a laugh. A servant as a friend to a lord? Then I thought of milady and our friendship. She was a queen and daughter of both a god and goddess, while I was the son of a second wife and fourth son. Yet that soon would change when Tanth was released. I just had to wait a little while longer for our plans to come forth.

"Of course, and she's your servant too?"

"Yes, my healer."

"One might think she tried to get away from you…" I said knowing how most humans felt about slaves running away.

"Her pony spooked, and I don't believe you would sell another…"

"Not all shifters are as nice or as loyal as the dogs of the north. I should know. Where I'm from many are killed and sold for power."

"Yet, you came here. Now let her go."

"You might be a lord, but-"

I stopped only to jump back. It seemed the wolf had decided that he wasn't going to wait anymore. I moved away, my hands letting go of the girl as I evaded the wolf's fangs. I then saw that the boy, Anwil, had grabbed the girl and pulled her close to him.

I smirked and started to fight with the wolf. I could feel all eyes on me, I knew why they were doing this. They wanted my power, they wanted to see my animal shape, and who was I not to show them. Besides it would give Tanth some more power to use.

I called forth the form I knew well. My clothes ripping as my skin was replaced with fur. Unlike what humans may think, a shifter changing is more like shedding skin. I stood there feeling the dirt between my paws. I then looked directly at the wolf, and he growled at me. I felt something around my neck.

So, milady's gift changed into a collar. I gave a soft purr knowing that I had the permission for milady to find and protect her sister. Though she did not tell me I couldn't have a little fun doing that. I could still feel the warmth from my seal now covered by fur. I could kill this shifter and then the rest. I would save milady's sister and have the last of Tanth's seal makers dead, and I would rule Sollin.

I was about to attack the wolf, but something caught both my attention and that of the wolf. The smell of blood and then footsteps. I growled; hunters. And they were looking for the man who burned the inn. I could not face them and this group together. Even though I am a prince, and gifted, I know my limits. I had to come up with a plan quickly.

I lowered myself to the ground and quickly transformed back.

"I believe hunters are about, how about we enact a truce until we have outrun them."

"Why should we believe you?" asked Gael.

"Because I know where the King of Dragons lies and where his mate sleeps."

I watched as the human's eyes widened, then he glanced at his servants. I could tell he was taking his time thinking about what he should do with me. I then saw dark mist almost unseen slip into his ear, his eyes seemed to flash and then he looked at me again.

"Very well, we will let you stay. You will lead us to the dragon and we will keep you way from the hunters."

"Very good. My name is Damion." I replied smiling at my luck once again and the power of my goddess.

## Anwil

I was surprised to see the lion before us submit. I was also surprised to see that Gael had agreed to it. I did not care though because Balder had gotten out his bow, And that meant that either there was game close or an enemy. I could tell by growls from Freki and Damion that it was enemy.

"Anwil, take Ingrid. I want you both ready to run."

"My lord…" I started I was no coward, and I would stand with him and the others.

"Anwil, you and Ingrid. She's a child no matter how old she seems."

"But the lion, how do we know that he will help you all."

"Don't argue with our lord, besides I will make sure the lion doesn't betray us." Balder stated as he grabbed an arrow from the quiver on his back.

I ground my teeth but obeyed. I got on my horse pulling Ingrid with me. After she was safely tucked between the horse and myself, I prepared myself to run if the need came. I did whisper a prayer to Fraia though. The goddess of the green and the goddess of my mother.

*"Please… I know have no right, but please protect them."*

I then felt a breeze and rustle of branches, I took that a sign that I was heard. I then looked down at the road before us, but before I could say anything the voice of my master filled the air.

"Go." His voice making both myself and the horse jump.

Then I went quickly away from them, my heart thundering in my chest as I ran like a thief with stolen treasure.

Π

I had laid Ingrid down on a blanket as I started a fire. We had made it a safe place, a small cave that was well hidden from the road. I had marked it though using a spell that Freki had taught me when I was young. All I had to do now was wait until our company came back.

I sighed when I saw nothing, I leaned back on the tall stone behind me. I felt a weight in my chest, my hands reached to bring out the only thing I had left from my childhood. The one thing that my mother and adoptive father had given me.

It was made from silver, the stone of elves and amber, the stone of the earth. The silver was shaped as roots which surrounded the amber inside it. The chain that I wore around my neck was made from deer hide, strengthened by a spell that was unknown to me.

I found myself closing my eyes and listening to the wind rustle through the trees. I was taken back to a time where I would always listen to it as a child. The music that would lull me to sleep along with the voices of those dear. I then felt wetness on my cheek, I opened my eyes and touched the tear.

"No time for me to miss it, no I can't…"

Yet I found myself listening to the wind as it whistled, a song that I could hear. I felt myself humming along, a memory calling me. I took a breath and looked up to the sky.

*"Mother of the earth, keeper of the woods, the knight of wild, the teacher of healers and a father's daughter. Come to heal and barter, to protect those she holds dear, with the magic that comes from the largest bear to the smallest hare. The one we call here...."*

*"To grace us with protection and knowledge to heal those we hold both in heart and fear."*

I looked to see that Ingrid was awake. I blushed at the thought that she must have heard me singing. I was going to say something when she spoke.

"A nature blessing. Did the last healer...."

"No, it was my mother...a long time ago."

"Oh...does it have to do with pedant around your neck?"

I looked down and moved my pedant back underneath my shirt. She sighed and looked around. Frowning a little as she saw it was just me and her. I sighed and started to explain.

"After your pony ran off we went looking for you. We found you in the company of a lion shifter."

"A lion shifter...but I though they are from Sollin?"

"Which is why it's weird that he would be here in Kadian." I replied gripping the earth.

"Didn't..." she started to ask but I stopped her.

The wind had shifted and I could smell something vile. It was almost enough to cause my breathing to stop. Then darkness surrounded us and I fell to the floor. The last thing I saw was Ingrid's eyes wide in fear.

**Ingrid**

My eyes widened as I watched Anwil fall like a rag doll. I turned to see a figure made of darkness…no not darkness, but shadows. My heart started to beat faster, my mind racing as the figure turned to me.

"Child of elfin heir, I have no order for you, but I must take the child of Linus."

"Linus?"

"You are not of his blood nor his mate, I will not tell you of that family."

"Then tell me who are you.."

"I am a servant of Erembour, the King of Shadows."

"Why would the king of death want a boy…."

"Because his family must pay a debt."

"What kind of debt would they have with…"

"I will not tell you child, for you are not one to know about it."

I was about to ask the figure more when a light filled the air. I watched as the figure moved away from it. I realized where the light was coming from- it was from his underneath Anwil's shirt. I watched as the shadow was pulled away and disappeared, only to be replaced by the footsteps of their party.

"Anwil, Ingrid?" Lord Gael stated as he ran into the opening of the cave.

"We're fine…" I replied a little shocked to see the man panting and worried about his slaves.

"Good…"

I found myself moving to Anwil, touching his body making sure nothing was broken. I sighed in relief, no broken bones or internal bleeding. I winced seeing the cut on his forehead.

"How bad?"

"Not too deep, though I need to clean it."

"Balder, get her bag."

Once I looked at the wound I whispered a small blessing. When I saw the wound glow a little, I reached into my bag and got out a needle and a thread. Once the glow cleared the wound, I started to stich.

"What attacked ya?" Freki asked.

"A servant of the King of Shadows." I replied trying to stop my body from shaking.

"Wow, so your party is strange, not only do you have a high ranked mix blood, but also a boy who's wanted by the death bringer." I looked over to see a southern shifter.

"You're the one that found me?" I asked not knowing why I was feeling uneasy seeing him.

"Damian Pridus."

"So, what is a son of the head clan of the south doing here?" I asked frowning.

"Helping a friend."

I nodded getting back to work. Once I deemed Anwil was okay, I went to the other members of our party. Balader and Freki were both covered in bumps and scrapes, but none were too bad. Lord Gael had a small cut on his wrist which I quickly bandaged.

"You're a little young for an elf healer." Damion asked

"I had to leave my master." I replied.

"Why?"

"She doesn't need to answer you." I heard Balder reply as he stood in front of me.

"Could it be that you are searching for someone you lost? A sister?"

I shivered, my mouth moving before I thought about what I was saying.

"Astrid, my sister was taken."

"By a dragon?"

"How?!" my heart was beating faster.

"She's the friend that I'm helping."

"Helping?"

"She asked me to find you, to make sure you're okay."

"How is she? The dragon hasn't hurt her, right?"

"She's safe, the dragon didn't harm her."

"But?" I said shaking.

"She's still under his spell."

I nodded, then I felt a hand on my shoulder. I looked to see that it was lord Gael. He gave me a reassuring smile and then started to speak.

"At least we know she's safe and we're close to where the dragon lives that took her."

"If you're heading up there to save her, you must know there's more than one dragon." Damion said.

"How many?"

"Five that can fight, and a small fledging."

"Fledging?" I asked.

"It's a child dragon." stated Anwil who had woken up.

"So, you know of dragons." Damion said with a smirk.

"I have experience."

"Very well, I will lead you to where I last saw Astrid. Is that fair?"

"What do you get in return?" I asked.

"I have already told your master what I want. Just some help keeping away hunters."
I shivered, I knew about hunters and I didn't like the image of them being close. Yet I couldn't help but feel that having Damion with us was even worse.

## Damion

I smiled as I rode at the front of the party I had joined. I made sure my mark was hidden, I didn't want anyone to know who I really worked for. The mark that helped me trick the lord and his servants followed him.

I caught a look of milady's sister. She was a beauty, even more than she had been described to me. I could watch her for hours but the pain in my mark told me I had other things to do first. I needed to break the seal. Then and only then I could make Ingrid my queen.

We had been riding for a few hours, everyone seemed on edge. It was the mark which was giving off this magic to the five around me. I smirked. If the magic leaked any more then it would be easier to trick and win them over.

"We all need a break, and the horses need a rest." I heard the lord say, as he got off his mount first.

The rest of us followed and we walked our steeds to the river that was close by. As the animals drank we all sat or in some cases laid down on the grass. I thought it was the best time to start my plan.

"Since were sitting here, let me tell you all a tale." I said as I sat on a log.

"I think we're all too old…." The elf Balder started.

"We all need to take our minds off what we're doing, if only for a little while," the lord replied, motioning for me to start my tale.

I smiled and relaxed as I started the tale of Tanth and her betrayal.

*"In the early years of the country of Sollin, two children were born to the ruler of the land. One, a beauty with dark hair and golden eyes, while the other was plain with dull brown and hair that was the same color. Their names were Tanth and Oria, the two daughters of the south.*

*The two girls grew and each passing day Tanth became a beauty while her sister stayed plain. The two finally reached the age of being married, their father went*

Whittney Corum

*to them to ask what their dowry for the men their mate
would be.*

*Tanth asked for a golden dress with jewels and
golden trinkets in the dress to show off her beauty. Oria
asked for a simple thread and needle, which caused
everyone in her family to laugh. Tanth though applauded
her sister and decided to help her.*

*Though she was tricked, for when she was trying on
her dress, her sister took the needle and thread and used it
to sew the beautiful girl up inside of it. Tanth could not get
out and before she could scream for help her sister used
magic to bind her mouth.*

*Once Oria was done, she took her sister into a cave
that was deep and dark. Tanth was then sealed alive. With
her sister sealed and gone Oria married the prince that had
been promised to her sister. Their children then became the
rulers of Sollin.*

*Though it's said that Tanth was able to send her
soul into a woman and bear a child of her own blood. That*

*child and his family are said to be the true rulers, the pure*
*bloods that will bring Sollin back to glory."*

"I've heard that story, but you seem to be missing parts." I looked at Anwil, who was shaking.

"Oh, and you know the story, a boy who's hiding something?" I asked.

"Yes…Tanth was beautiful on the outside, but not I her heart. She tried to kill her own sister for the throne…"

I smirked, as everyone turned their head to look at Anwil. They were surprised that he knew about my story. I felt my mark ooze in pleasure.

"How do you know that story?"

"My mother…."

"Your mother?" The four of them asked as one.

"How would your mother know the story?" I asked, with fake amazement.

I watched as the boy finally broke, the questions became too much. I had to hold back a laugh when I watched how he shook, his eyes on me.

"My mother's name was Alatea, she was the heir of Oria...she told me of how Tanth tried to steal the throne and tried to become a goddess."

I smirked and nodded.

"That may be true, but why would your mother run from Sollin?"

"I don't..."

"I do, because in the years after sealing of Tanth your family became lustful for power. You killed those who weren't supportive of you. I heard your mother even killed her promised mate to run off with some unnamed shifter, who left..."

"My mother was kind.... a healer..."

"Even healers can kill...."

"Leave him be." I heard a voice and looked to see that Ingrid was standing between us.

"So, you have a champion," I spoke, a little annoyed that my promised queen would stand up for the boy.

"I just think you shouldn't speak…"

"Does everyone know what happened after she left our kingdom? How she found your adoptive father after the real one left you? Do they know what he was and what you did to them both?"

"I…didn't…" the boy started to crack.

"I wonder how everyone would react knowing what blood you have on your hands."

"What in the world are you talking about?" Lord Gael asked, standing up. I could feel his anger.

"Your servant, Anwil. The child of a princess and adoptive son of a dragon, killed them."

I watched as everyone's faces were in shock. True they hunted dragons, but this was first time that they heard of him being raised by one. I watched as he ran into the bushes.

I was surprised when Ingrid followed him, although if they are alone together then I would only have to deal with these three first. I felt my mark glow as I walked toward them, their backs turned to me. Yes, I was so close to wearing a crown. I wouldn't care the color of jewels, red as blood.

## Anwil

*Why was I running? Why didn't I speak up? Why? Why?*

The thoughts were running through my head as I followed a path in the woods. I didn't know why hearing a story my mother told me so long ago would force me to act. The way Damion told it, I should of known he wanted this reaction. He wanted the others to know of my past, but why?

I was so busy thinking that I didn't see the tree in front of me. I tripped over its roots and found myself face first in the mud. I flipped over and laid on my back catching my breath. I felt my eyes sting with the start of tears, tears that I hadn't cried in years.

"The one wound that my master didn't tell me how to heal...a broken heart." I looked up see Ingrid.

Her hair was wild, and her clothes were dirtied and ripped. She must have followed me when I ran. I sighed and sat up and she knelt. I didn't say anything at first but then I heard the winds whisper through the trees.

"Your mother was a shifter who believed in Faia."

"The goddess blessed her when she was younger." I found myself saying.

"And your birth father?"

"He was healer and shifter also…but he wasn't in a clan."

"But every shifter is in a clan…my papa told me even if a shifter was an orphan."

"Yes, but my father was not from the four brothers."

"But all clans…"

"My mother told me once that shifters had forgotten something when they told the first shifters."

"What is it?"

"That the four brothers had a sixth sibling. A small child that gained the ability not to shift into animals like the brothers. No, it was so different and crazy that the brothers were wondering if Flickron was drunk when doing it…"

"Doing what?"

"Giving a child the ability to transform into any person they wish."

I watched as the information fell into her mind. Trying to figure out what I was saying, then I remembered a tale my uncle told us once of the sister of the four brothers.

That the child was born without the ability to transform like her brothers. She was loved by them though, but she also had a twin that lived in the shadows. Some say that he was born the spitting image of the girl but slowly changed to a darker version of her.

It was said he had tricked many people by transforming himself in his twin and brothers. Yet it came to a head when he was in his sister's form and killed her suitor. The girl pleaded for her life as she was sentence to death for the killing. It was only with help from Flickron that the girl survived and was transformed into a minor goddess of women. The man became the most hated shifter of all.

"A spirit shifter…"

"Yes, but in Sollin they call them Empusa, since they believe that when they shift, they use the blood of who they transform into."

"Do they?"

"No…at least most don't."

"Most?"

"My father once killed a man to take his face…so he could survive."

"Which explains why the King of Shadows is after you."

I laughed and looked to the sky.

"That's funny to you?"

"The king doesn't care about what a healer did to save his own skin. My mother told me my ten times grandfather cheated death many times by switching his face with others."

"So the King of Death is after you because he couldn't find his prey, and you're laughing about it." she replied with a frown.

"Yeah, I guess I just feel if he comes to get me now, that he's collecting what he's owed." I replied touching my necklace.

"After all I have caused so many deaths already...."

"You're too young to think about death."

We both looked to see a woman who was dressed in a plant-like dress with tanned skin, her hair a mixture of white, black and gold. My grip tightened and I watched as the woman, who was walking close to the woods seemed to be glowing.

"Lady Faia." I whispered as she smiled at the both of us.

"I have come to speak the child of Lea and sister of the Dragon Queen."

Whittney Corum

## Ingrid

"You're the voice from my dream…"

"Yes, though you didn't take it the way that I thought you would."

"I don't…"

"Most don't understand my visions, those who do are sometimes called mad."

I nodded, and then looked behind her to see a white stag. Faia must have seen me looking and motioned for the beast to come over towards us. Once it was close I reached out my hand to touch it. I could feel the heartbeat of the animal and closed my eyes to hear the song of the stag's heart.

"It seems Pan knows that your dear to Astrid."

"You know my sister?"

"You're definitely the child of shifter and elf. Both kinds are very protective of their families." She said with a smile.

Then I realized who I was talking to. I knelt and bowed my head. I started to mutter apologies when I felt a hand on my head.

"Easy, little one. I know how it feels to worry about a sister."

I felt comfort in her words and looked up into her eyes. I could see warmth in them but also sadness. It seemed that the lady was worried about something and I wanted to know why. Before I could think about it longer, my mouth opened and I began to speak.

"Lady Faia…"

She shook her head and walked away from us. I heard Anwil stand up and come over to me. When he put his hand on my shoulder the goddess started to speak.

"I called you two here to speak to you about the path ahead."

"The path?" I heard Anwil ask.

"Yes, you two have been following a false one."

The trees seemed to move, and leaves danced around us. Then they started to form pictures, as if they were puppets behind a screen. I watched as a figure appeared, rounded with child, a dragon before her.

"Your sister is with child, the child who has dragon blood."

"That monster…"

"The child was made because of true love, but others have been led to think it hasn't."

"But…" I found myself trying to say something.

The picture showed my sister rubbing her belly as an elder man stood before her. He seemed to be frowning. I couldn't help but feel worry coming from him. I felt myself feeling the same way too.

"Your sister's children are in danger, by some part of your own selfishness."

"I…" started but stopped seeing the look in the goddess's eye.

"Ingrid, I understand why you would think your sister is in danger, she is. But I wouldn't think she would want you close when the battle comes."

"Battle?"

"Yes, the battle that will end a line."

"What line?" Anwil asked with a frown.

"That I cannot tell you Anwil…" The goddess replied gently.

"Is it my master?"

"Anwil…"

"Haven't I already lost enough? Haven't my hands had enough blood on them?" I looked at him to see that he had tears in his eyes.

"Child, the only blood you have spilled was an accident."

I was about to say something, but the leaves started the show another scene. It was a cave and inside was a woman at a spinning wheel. Running in was a younger Anwil and beside him was a man with yellow tattoos.

"Brenna, the daughter of Bran, and the mother of Anwil."

"She's with a dragon…"

"My second father." Anwil whispered.

I didn't say anything, I just watched as the scene changed. Now the young Anwil was in the arms of his master's father. While the bodies of his mother and second

father were on the floor. The boy was crying reaching out
to the bodies.

"What…"

"Anwil, you are not at fault for the death of your
parents, a traitor chose to use you as a way of killing them."
Faia stated as she walked over. The visions disappeared.

"I didn't stop it though…"

"A child shouldn't be a protector of their parents.
Though sometimes it seems they believe they need to be."

"Lady Faia…" I started.

"The one who tricked you back then was a follower
of Tanth, the mother of the one that you now travel with."

Then the leaves moved and showed the figure of the
lion that was now with our group. My mouth went wide as
the goddess kept talking. I thought I heard rage in her
voice.

"A shifter who has used a friend's trust to betray her but also to help her. He will try to have her and you both as his wives. "

"Why?"

"Because he wants to rule his homeland and the only way to do that is to release his ancestor Tanth. Her freedom for his rule and the only way to do it is to kill the last of her sister's line."

Her eyes went to Anwil and then I realized what she was saying. Anwil was the last of the line of the woman who sealed Tanth away. I watched as he shook and then I reached over and took his hand. He relaxed and I found myself smiling a little.

"You two need to tread carefully, your lives and the ones you hold close are in danger also." Faia stated.

"I know…"

"Child, you may think you know, but not everything is known to one person. Not even I know everything."

"Lady…."

"That's why it's wise to work together, for one's knowledge might be the helper for one who doesn't know anything."

I nodded as the goddess of the wood walked over to Anwil and touched the necklace he was wearing. It started to grow and the vines started to warp and grow stronger.

"I gave this to your ancestor a long time ago. It's a heart of the last Sun tree of Sollin. The rest were killed by Tanth because she wanted the soil to make her own castle. Call forth it's power, for it's the one thing that can seal her back if she would be released."

"But how…"

"When Tanth was first sealed away her sister had help from another shifter, elf, and human."

"A trio like that…."

"Was very different during those times, though it seems their heirs seemed to find each other again."

"My master, Balder, and Freki …"

"Yes."

"Wait, we left them with that lion…." I started.

"Then you all must head back."

I nodded as the goddess made a doorway. Anwil went first and I was going to follow but I felt a hand on my shoulder. I looked into the goddess's eyes, and I could tell she was worried.

"Ingrid, you're from a great line of healers, but I am afraid that will not be enough."

"Because I stopped training?" I asked shaking.

"Partly."

"The other part?"

"Your magic is being twisted by your feelings."

"My feelings?"

"The feelings that your sister needs…"

"She might be with child…that doesn't mean that the dragon put a spell on her."

"Child…very well, I can see the only way for you to face this is by talking to your sister…but before you go I will give you a gift."

"A gift?"

She called forth magic into a green orb then walked over to me. I felt my own healing magic reach out it. As the orb was consumed by my magic the goddess started to speak.

"The spell I'm giving you is a strong one, it's meant for those I deem worthy of it. It was crafted by both myself and the Shadow King."

I froze the only spell I knew that the King of Death and Faia worked on was the one spell that every healer was determined to know. The spell that could bring breath back to those who were at death's door.

"The shadow healing…"

"Yes, but be warned, you can only use this spell three times. Any more than that and your soul will be owed to the King. Also, if you should do more knowing that, those of your line will be chosen to take on the debt."

"Like Anwil…"

"Yes, Though I have been speaking to the king about him, he still hasn't yielded to me yet."

"Yielded?" I asked as the goddess blushed a little.

"Just go my dear, you all must get to your sister soon. I fear for her and children."

## Damion

I was left alone with the elf, wolf shifter, and human as my prey when my mistress's sister left. I smirked knowing that this was going to make my life a little easier. I needed all three of them to release the seal.

So I called forth my magic to knock them out. I heard the sound of wings, and I looked up to see Alik with two other dragons. I smiled as the dragon looked at the three sleeping bodies.

"Who are these?"

"They are ones who have been killing dragons. The king needs to put them trial."

I watched as the dragon nodded and picked up the three. I caught a ride with them and couldn't wait to tell Lady Astrid what I had found out. I couldn't wait for her to whisper in her mate's ear what I had found out...or what I wanted her to tell him.

□

I was watching as the King and Queen of Dragons spoke. Blagdon was frowning as Astrid pace back and forth. She was close to giving birth to their child.

"Astrid…"

"Ingrid, goddess what are ya thinking."

"I don't know if she was forced or not to go with these three, and I did try to save her." I replied.

"Yes, but she's still with one of these…these…"

"Murderers?" I asked.

"Yes…"

"Astrid, please sit down, yer worrying me and you have been told to rest." Blagdon said as he walked over and placed her on a chair.

"But…"

"I will get to the bottom of this, we're going to have the three tried for their crimes. I will ask them where your sister is also."

I hid a smirk; everything was falling into place. I knew the way the that the dragon's held a trial. They usually took the blood of the accused placed it in a bowl which showed the memories of the person. Yet with a simple spell the bowl could be used as a portal. I would use that portal to open the seal so my mistress can be released.

I stood up and walked over to the two and bowed. I gave back the cloak that lady Astrid gave me, and it changed into a blanket to cover her. Once she relaxed, I took a breath and went into the lines that were given to me by my mistress.

"My lord and lady be warned these three are cold hearted killers of dragons. They will lie to protect each other. I think you to use silence spell to keep two quiet while other speaks."

I watched them nodding, again I had to hide my smirk. Soon I would rule over my own kingdom and would have two queens and the control of dragons. I followed the King of Dragons, bidding Lady Astrid goodbye.

Once we were out of earshot I spoke with Blagdon.

"The fourth man is using Ingrid, she's innocent for the most part."

"I know that…but the council will have to judge her too."

"Not if you give her a pardon, pledge her to your son."

He stopped and looked at me. I could see his eyes give a green hue filled with protectiveness. I then felt myself being pushed to the wall because of the strength coming from him.

"Ya are overstepping yer bounds boy, even though my flera might allow you to be a messenger yer nothing to me. You can play yer games with others, but I remind ya dragons are greedy. So, when someone tried to take something or hurt something precious to us, ya going to be in a world of pain, that ye will want the King of Shadows to take ya."

"Of course, your highness…"

"Ye make sure that you keep your ideas to yerself."

I nodded as he dropped me to the floor. I caught my breath and saw him stand over me. I looked up as he growled.

"Ya might know a wee bit about our ways, but ya have no right to speak of things that don't concern ya."

With that he left me to think about his words. Once he was out of sight I smiled. I had riled his blood. I knew that those who had their blood boiling will make rash decisions. I felt my mark burn, I knew it was because she was ready to be free.

"Soon mistress…soon you'll help me claim my throne."

"And you'll free me from the seal." I heard her whisper as I walked into the cave where the trial was taking place.

Anwil

I felt the fire before Ingrid came out the portal.
When she did I pushed her down as the fire went over us.
Once it was done he looked up to see a small dragon. It was
a fledging with green scales and dark gold on his belly. His
green eyes looking at us, and I put Ingrid behind me.

"Anwil is that…."

"A fledging, a couple of years old…"

"Oh…"

I nodded looking around, if there is a fledgling here
then a parent would be close or at least another dragon. I
cursed when I heard a growl and we both looked to see a
woman heavily pregnant and magic coming off her. Before
we could do anything the dragon went over to the woman.

Once he was next to her, he was wrapped in a fire ball  and
when the flames died, a small boy appeared. The woman
pushed him behind her as she growled at us. I pushed

Whittney Corum

Ingrid behind me, I didn't know how much magic this
woman had but we had entered the nesting area where her
child was.

"Who are ya, and what are ya doing here?"

"I'm Anwil…we didn't mean to come here…we mean no
harm the fledgling."

"Yet why are you here? Who sent ya?"

"I…."

"Astrid?" I heard Ingrid cry out, running to the woman.

"Ingrid?" the woman asked as she pulled Ingrid into a hug.

"Mama?"

"Aiden, this is your Aunt Ingrid…"

"Aunt Ingrid?" Both the boy and Ingrid stated.

Astrid sighed then looked back at me. I stood straight up and readied myself for an attack. Yet I was surprised when I heard her voice filled with kindness. It was as if a gently rain had started to fall.

"Anwil was your name, right? I don't know if I should kill you for bringing my sister to death or thank you for bringing her to me."

"What do you mean death…."

"You have killed many dragons and some of the council believe my sister should be judged with you and the rest of your company."

"Wait my master and the others are here?" I asked standing up.

"Yes, they're to be judge by the high council of dragons…"

"Is it a true trial or are they walking to their deaths?" I growled looking at her.

"There's a saying in shifter kind, those who bring blood will have blood taken."

"There is also one that says a trail of madness starts with revenge." Ingrid said as she crossed her arms.

Astrid sighed and patted the boy's hair and rubbed her belly. She looked at me and I felt like I was seeing my own mother, though it only lasted a second. I felt myself relaxing as she started to speak again.

"Very well, I will lead ya to the council chamber, and will try to talk to them to clear their heads."

"Thank…"

She stopped me with her hand.

"Don't thank me, you still have blood on yer hands, blood of the council's friends and family. If they do calm down ya still will be facing punishment."

"I know, but at least it will be fair…"

"But what about the lion?" I heard Ingrid ask.

"Lion, ya mean Damion…" Astrid replied with a gentle smile.

"Astrid, he's a traitor. Not just to us but to you also."

I watched as Astrid's face turned into a confused frown as the boy shivered.

"*Liar!*" The boy stated, trying to attack but was stopped by his mother.

"Aiden we do not bite. We'll speak of this in my chambers, Damion is a messenger but also a friend."

"A friend that you sent to find Ingrid, he told us."

"Yes…"

"Do you also know he's of southern blood and serves Tanth?"

"Who's Tanth?"

"A woman who betrayed not just her land but her family." I remarked frowning.

"And how do you…"

"Because he comes from the family that she betrayed." Ingrid said as she touched my shoulder.

I felt relief and calmness going through my veins. I then looked at Astrid whose gaze seemed to soften a little. Then we felt the ground shake, I pushed Ingrid to the wall as Astrid grabbed it also. To my surprise some her cloak transformed into rope to help keep the women in place.

"Astrid, how do dragons hold a trial?"

"They use the blood of the accused to see if they're telling the truth…"

"We need to get to the chamber that houses the trial." I said, as I started to move.

"Wait, you would go into a chamber that you know nothing of?"

"To help my master and friends, yes."

"Have you ever hunted?"

"What has that…."

"When hunting, one needs to know the area where yer hunting."

"We don't have…"

"Then make…Oh goddess…" Astrid stated as she winced.

"What?"

"My water just broke…"

My eyes went wide along with Ingrid, she quickly went to her sister's side while I went to the other side of the pregnant elfin-shifter. We took her to a small cave, the young dragon following after us.

"What the matter with my mama?"

"She's going to give birth to your little sibling."

The boy's eyes went wide, and he grabbed his mother's hand. She gave him a strained smile and then cursed as the earth shifted again. I decided then what I had to do. I turned to Ingrid and shouted.

"Take them somewhere safe."

"What are you going to do?"

"Save my master and the men who raised me."

"By yourself?"

"Your sister needs your help."

"But…"

"Why are you hesitating? Isn't this what you wanted to find? Your sister? To get revenge on the dragon who took her?"

"Yes…"

"Then you should leave with her, at least then you'll be away from all this. You can go live the life you want now."

"But…"

I didn't answer her. I pushed her and the other two away into a portal that was behind them. I could feel that whoever made the portal was there to help the three. Yet when I pushed Ingrid my necklace fell from my neck and into her hand. I sighed. If I was going to die anyway I wouldn't need the pendant.

## Ingrid

We landed in a small clearing and I looked at my hand to see the pendant. How was Anwil going to fight and seal the traitor? I heard a gasp and I went back to my sister who was about to give birth.

"Astrid…" I started as I noticed that she was pale.

"I'm fine, it hurts…"

"Well, you are having a child…"

A child that was going to be half dragon with both shifter and elfin blood flowing though it's veins. It seemed she heard what I thought and frowned before she screamed in pain. I looked to see that blood was seeping from her.

"You got hurt…"

"Yeah, a piece of falling rock caught my back…"

"I need to…"

"My child needs more help then I."

"But…."

"I know you were learning to be a healer…didn't your teacher tell you…"

"That when it comes to births, the baby is first task…but this is different you're bleeding…"

"Ingrid Sara Finnis, you will help my baby then you will help me, or so help me I will haunt ya for the rest of your life." The last part was a mixture of yell and growl.

"Okay…" I replied feeling the magic coming off her.

I started a prayer to the healer spirits and to the goddess to help me. I was surprised though when I felt a hand on my shoulder. I then felt a warmth that filled my body.

"Leave this to me young elf, your needed elsewhere." I looked up to see Faia.

"But…"

"I will tend to your sister and the gifts she carries."

"Gifts…"

"SEVEN STARS, IT HURTS."

We both winced, and she gave me a look with a mixture of empathy and seriousness. I found myself biting my lip but nodded as she smiled, then gently took the pendant and put it across my neck. It felt as if a weight was being put on my shoulders.

"Good, now go back to Anwil. He needs a clear head to help him."

I frowned and bit my lips, a clear head? My head wasn't clear. I felt a hand on my head and felt my thoughts slow as a voice calmed me down.

"Clear your mind, use the seed to find Anwil and seal the traitor before she gains more power. Also remember your gift, remember the price of a third time."

"I know." I whispered as I ran into the portal, sparing a glance at my sister who gave me a smile.

I made a promise to myself that I would come back to her and see the child that was going to be born. Yet as I left through the portal I remembered what Faia stated, gifts…did that mean that my sister was having more than one baby? I shook my head I would find out after I saved Anwil and the others who helped me get here.

☐

I found myself back in the caves, but one thing was different. The caves were still, almost like someone or something stopped their shaking. I shivered, the only beings that could have that power would be an elemental user who was born with powerful magic, or an immortal.

The only immortal I knew that would be in the caves was the one that sealed away. Tanth was free and all the lives in this cave were forfeit, I hoped I wouldn't be the first life that would be taken.

Whittney Corum

**Damion**

I smiled, standing beside my mistress as the dragons and men were brought to the floor. My eyes watching as red flowed like little streams on the ground below us. I could feel power running though me, a reward for bringing her here.

"You've done well my little lion."

"Thank you."

"Yet I see were missing one."

"He'll come."

"He better, I want to get this done, then we will claim what is yours and mine."

I nodded as I heard footsteps, my mistress smiled and called forth her powers.

"The foolish boy has come to his death."

I watched as Anwil came into the main cave. My mouth turning to a smile when he saw his friends on the floor. He went to their aid, as if he could help the three. I then turned my attention to the dragons.

They were bounded by chains made my mistress, as they struggled to get free the bonds would tighten. My eyes fell on the King of Dragons, his scales turning bright red from his struggling. His eyes looked straight at mine, a mixture of anger and fear. I knew the anger was directed at me, while the fear was for his mate, child, and the child yet to be born.

I heard a groan and looked to see Anwil helping the human get up. I looked at my mistress who nodded and I got out my dagger. I jumped off the pillar we were standing on and walked over to the shifter and his master.

"You are a fool aren't you?"

"At least I'm a fool who honors my ties, you broke yours. Why? Because of some need that your craving?"

"You can call it that, I call it taking my place as the true ruler of Sollin."

"And how many lives is the crown worth to you? Will it ever stop or is your goal even higher?"

"You mean to become a god? Yes, that thought had come to me. Both my mistress and I will be better off if I am to stay a king. A king who would take the world into my own hands."

"You think that three goddesses or the northern gods will allow that?"

"They don't have a choice; my mistress is now free, and she is just as powerful."

"Yet she was one who was sealed away…"

"Yes, but we're going to make sure that doesn't happen again."

"Even if you kill me there might be…"

"Others? Anwil you're the only child of your traitor mother. Her family was killed leaving only her and you. You're the last of your line."

"The last…"

I readied my dagger to attack him when a group of vines comes between us. I jumped away and then looked over to see that Ingrid was running toward us, one hand out in front of her controlling the vines while the other cradled something to her chest. My eyes widened; how did she have the seed? I thought all the trees that helped seal my mistress were destroyed. I growled, knowing if she got close to Anwil or his other friends, that they would have a chance to seal my mistress back. I couldn't let that happen, so I jumped over the vines and threw my knife at her. My vision filled with red as I heard a scream come from both Anwil and Ingrid.

## Anwil

"Balder!" I screamed as I watched the blond elf falling into Ingrid's arms.

I watched it all happen as if it were a dream, the knife was going to hit Ingrid in the chest ending her and the seed. Then Balder jumped between the two, the knife burying into his back. He groaned into pain, I noticed that the blade was in to the hilt.

"Why?" I heard Ingrid ask.

"Children…even those who lost their way…need to be…protected…"

"Don't talk I need…"

"Don't…it's my time…. don't waste a spell on someone…who has…no regrets…leaving…this life…"

"But what about those you love? What about Anwil and your master?"

"They…will….be fine…and you…Ingrid…one of the children of the high king…you are…you are worthy of that line…even…more than you know…" I watched as Balder touched the seed in Ingrid's hand and it started to glow. He then looked over at me.

"Now…it's…time…to finish…what our…ancestors…started…"

His hand fell as he closed his eyes for the last time. I felt tears fall from my own face as one of men who raised me left the world. Then my eyes went to the seed that Ingrid was holding. It was glowing, as if Baldar's last breath had awakened it.

"Anwil.." I looked down to my master.

His wounds were minor, but he was also weak. I felt myself shiver seeing the once strong leader brought down by wounds and shock. I then felt another person in front of us, and I looked at Ingrid.

"He's going to be okay…I can tell that…"

"Good."

She looked behind us and bit her lip. I glanced over and could see why she was worried. The vines which came to our aid were being weeded away by Damion. Then my eyes went to Tanth, her eyes were looking at the dragons as her spells held them down. I then looked at the seed.

The said seed was glowing in a steady heartbeat, it's glow calling out me. I then saw the glow touch my master and his breathing eased. The seed started to glow brighter. Then a light reached over to the knocked out Freki who was in his wolf form. I felt it reaching out towards me, I felt something racing in me also. I took a breath then took the seed and stood up, looking at Ingrid.

"Stay with Freki and Master, make sure they live."

"What are you going to do?"

"Finish what my mother's line started." I stated as I looked over to the Tanth.

"But…"

"Just do as I say." I yelled and watched her bite her lips.

I turned my back to her, the seed following my heartbeat.

"Listen, once I have Tanth's attention, the dragons will be free. I don't know if they'll attack us or not, but in case they do recite a protection spell…"

"What about you?"

"I'll be fine."

"Don't lie, your risking your life…"

"I know, but there are some things worth risking your life for."

"I know…"

"So, shut up, and let me do what I need to do."

I didn't hear her answer as I jumped from vines and her and went to the woman who caused my mother's death. My heart and seed beating, ready to seal the darkness once again. A darkness who's reach is longer than her own hands, which I realized as I felt a pain in my back.

**Ingrid**

"Anwil!" I shouted as I watched Damion's dagger buried
into Anwil's back.

My body was frozen as I watched the scene before me.
Anwil pulled the dagger out, a grimace on his face. He
turned to Damion, the dagger still in his hands. I heard the
voice of someone behind me.

"The price is close to being paid."

"The price…you meant the price his mother's ancestor
asked to seal Tanth?"

"The seed of a soul to seal a darkness that was brought into
the world, A child born of one of ancient foul gods and an
unfaithful queen. My master helped the true heir seal the
darkness away, though she feared that others would unseal
the darkness."

"So, she offered her blood line?"

"She thought that it would save her home, and for a while it did…"

"Yet, you followed Anwil…"

"Because of his father's line, the price came to him."

I wanted to scream. Why did one person have to lose their life, not because of what they did but because of what their family did. I looked at the shadow and bit my lip. How could I stop this, and if I did, would it be right? My body seemed to move on its own and I found myself whispering a spell.

"By the power of the green and the moon that is ever seen, protect the man before me, the child of the chosen Queen."

I watched as green light surrounded Anwil's body healing his wound. He looked at me and nodded and he went back to his plan to attack the traitor. I felt someone push me down as something sharp flew by.

"Keep you head down."

Whittney Corum

I looked up and saw that Freki had gotten up and pushed me down. I saw that he also had a cut from the dagger that was supposed to have hit me.

"Why?"

"You're a child…I can't let ya die."

"What about…"

"Anwil knows what he's doing, believe in him."

"His life…"

"Is his, and your life is yours, and I will make sure that you can live it."

"You're not…"

"I needed a rematch, and I need to keep the lion away from Anwil."

"Anwil told me to…"

"Watch over me. Sometimes a pup needs to keep in mind who they are in the pack."

"But you're still hurt, as a healer…"

"As a wolf and your elder I say I need to help."

Before I could say anything else, a gray wolf jumped from the vines and landed in front of Damion. I bit my lip watching the lion and wolf attack each other. Then my eyes turned to Anwil, and my heart almost stopped.

Anwil had gotten close to Tanth and the woman spied him and was using a spell to keep him away. I felt helpless, how could I help two people at once. I felt tears sting at the sides of my eyes. I then felt someone else touch my shoulder.

"Ease little one, worry about the boy. I will take care of my own." I looked up to into golden eyes.

"Flickron…" I whispered as the god of shifters left my side and went to Freki

Whittney Corum

I then felt myself turn to Anwil who was now fighting Tanth. I started to whisper a spell.

"Grow those of green in the earth, grow and show how strong your bloom is worth."

Vines and rose blooms wrapped around Tanth making her lose focus as she tried to cut them away. I bit my lip feeling every cut. This spell was usually used for protection, but it did have a cost. Any damage to the blooms or vines would cause pain to the caster.

"Foolish child." Was what I heard before I felt my body scream in pain.

Tanth was burning the vines and the blooms and my body was on fire. All I felt was pain, my heart raging in my chest. It was almost too much I felt myself fall and darkness filled my vison.

## Damion

I was fighting against the wolf when another joined him. I growled, I knew who it was because I used to work for him. The god of all shifters, the trickster of the northern gods. I also knew what could get under his skin.

"Hello, Lord."

"Don't you even start you traitor." the white wolf growled.

"I stayed loyal to what I believe in…"

"Ya brought back a woman who has killed many…"

"She's my blood, she raised me…"

"She has poisoned ya, and you are too blind to see it."

I growled and launched at him, I could feel the power of my mistress fill me as I cut the god. He growled and jumped away I smiled seeing silver blood fall from his shoulder. I saw that the gray wolf shiver but still growled.

"So, you have given up on your own life…by using magic which taints your own blood."

"The blood that proves that I'm the rightful heir to the throne. I can save my land."

"Fool, that's not going to save yer land, you brought death to it, even I know that." The grey wolf stated as he came over to attack me.

"I don't need advice from a wolf who has no business in my affairs." I roared and attacked the grey wolf.

I smirked as I felt the power inside me and felt the taste of blood on my tongue. Then I heard the scream of Ingrid and smirked as the two wolves looked over at her. I ran to attack them only to feel a shield placed between us. I growled until I saw who oversaw the shield.

"Astrid." I heard the white wolf call out.

"You dare to betray us?" the Queen of Dragons growled.

I looked at the shifter who I had been serving, her hair loose and she seemed winded. Her belly now empty and her skin paler than usual. I growled, so she had given birth and the cub wasn't near.

"I thought shifters were taught to stay with their young." I taunted.

"My children are safe, I have come to protect my family." she stated.

Whittney Corum

"Then you have failed. Your mate is in chains and your sister…"

"SILENCE." I moved back as a knife was thrown at me.

"I hit a nerve didn't I." I taunted.

"Astrid, go to your sister." Flickron barked.

"But…"

"Go."

I watched as the queen transform into a snow-white wolf and ran to her sister. I went to stop her, only to be attacked by the bigger white and gray wolf. I showed my fangs and started to fight with them again. I stopped though when I heard the scream of my mistress.

Anwil

I clutched my side as I tried to get up from the spot that Tanth pushed me. The traitor growled as she tried to claw out the seed that was stuck to her side with the dagger that was once in my back. I felt faint, since my wound had opened when Ingrid was knocked out.

"Fool. Like my sister, your life would have been saved if you had joined me…"

"Yeah and become a shadow under your control."

"You could of helped rule this world…"

"Power isn't everything, loyalty and kindness are." I replied felling blood pour out of me.

"What about loyalty to your family?"

"You aren't my family."

"I'm from your blood…"

"Blood isn't the only thing that makes family, it's bonds…"

"Bonds! You lay there dying and no one comes to help you." She hissed.

"They're away from you…I can…at least make sure you…. don't harm anyone else…"

I watched as roots started come from the ground and wrap around her. She tried to move but the seed stopped her as it wrapped around her arms. I watched as she looked at me with a killing glare, only for it to disappear beneath the wood of the trunk.

I smiled as I closed my eyes, the darkness calling me.

X

I was standing in a throne room, my eyes on the figure sitting in front of me. The man was dressed in all back, his skin as pale as winter. His eyes were deep ruby and was looking at me with interest. I swallowed as I bowed and addressed the man.

"King Erembour…"

"Anwil, the child who payed a double price from both families."

"At least Tanth is sealed…"

"Yes, though your fate is up in the air still."

"What do you mean isn't this…."

"You're between worlds, and a goddess has championed you."

"Faia…but why?"

"Your mother was a good friend, and she believes that you shouldn't bear all the weight of your family debt."

"So?"

"Your life will last, but you must pay a price."

"What is it?" I felt a shiver run through me as the King of Death smiled.

"You'll become one of my servants, you will collect the spirits of those who have died and bring them here."

I swallowed and took a breath.

"And that will be my new life?"

"Somewhat. You can still have a wife and family if you wish, but when I call you, you must come."

"If I refuse?"

"Then you go to your final place and stay there."

"Do I even..."

"Boy, you have a second chance for a life, it might be different then what you had before. Take it before I decide that Faia's favor was wasted on you."

I simply nodded, I had a feeling that this was my fate. Then I looked at the king and found myself asking.

"Could I see her?"

"Your mother? I will give you a few moments, then you will start your new job."

"Thank you."

"Don't." he replied.

I then watched as smoke blew into the room and formed into a body. Standing in front of me was my mother. She was just as beautiful as I remembered, her dark hair piled on top of her head and her golden eyes looking at me.

"Anwil...my sweet boy."

"Mother...I.."

"We don't have much time love; your family is waiting for you."

I felt tears fall down my face as I embraced the woman before me.

"I'm sorry."

"I know little one, but it wasn't your arrow that took me nor magic. It was a man who tricked you into rivaling us."

"But you both died…"

"Yet you were safe, and you have been good."

"Mother, I killed dragons…"

"Yes, but you saved many a fledging and a flare or flera."

"But…"

"Anwil, you were following orders and I know that the lord you served tried to make sure the dragons he hunted were menaces…though sometimes you were tricked."

"Mom…"

"Now go, you have a new mission, and please be careful." She then hugged me before she disappeared.

"Now boy, come here." The king of darkness told me, and I obeyed.

"You swear to guide those spirits who leave their bodies in the natural world?"

"I do."

"Then I grant you the power of a spirit guide, and all the powers that go with it."

I felt magic fill my body as the symbol of the King of Death was etched into my skin. The symbol of a raven flying. I fell to my knees as I felt the power course through me.

"I know it's new power, but do stand up."

I did and suddenly my body felt better and I looked at the king who gave me a sad smile.

"Welcome to the fold my boy, now go back and I recommend you get ready for a scolding."

I tried to ask what he was talking about when I felt myself being pulled away again.

X

"Come on, breath stupid." I heard the voice of Ingrid pleading as I opened my eyes.

"Ingrid…"

"Stupid, stupid, what were you thinking, you almost died…"

"What happened…"

"You were heading toward the shadow land, lad." Freki stated, a tired smile on his face.

"But the elf child help you." Flickron replied as he then went over to Astrid.

"What…"

"I used the spell Faia gave, the one I can only used three times."

"Why?"

"Because you were dying."

"But why, you don't know me…"

"Maybe, but you have helped me out a lot getting here, you saved me the sale block…so I owed you one."

"Where's the lion?"

"Disappeared when the dragons were freed, we don't know where he went."

Whittney Corum

"Where's my lord?"

"He's resting, like you should be, the dragons have offered to shelter us for a few days until we recover." Ingrid replied as she touched my head.

"They will do that for us?"

"Well, we did take the queen to safety…"

"Yeah, how is your sister by the way?"

"Getting her own scolding, it seems after giving birth she rushed in to help us."

"But you're glad she's okay."

"Yeah, now close your eyes, it's time to rest."

I nodded closing my eyes and falling asleep feeling at rest.

## Ingrid

I watched as my sister held her babies, twins, a boy and girl. The first was a boy with my sisters' stock white hair and his father's dark green eyes. They had named the boy, Almod.

The other babe was a girl with a mix of black and red locks like her father. She had her mother's eyes. She is quieter then her brothers and named, Aisling.

I watched as my sister kissed her twins as the King of Dragons came in. He smiled and kissed my sister and then twins then looked at me. I could still see the uncertainty in his eyes. I don't blame him, I did come here to save my sister by any means.

"So, what are your plans Ingrid?"

"Blagdon." My sister warned.

"It's okay Astrid, he's right. I should decide what to do."

My sister sighed and laid back on her pillows, she was on bedrest after giving birth to twins. It didn't help that she had jumped into the fight with Tanth, so she was confined to quarters for a few months. I was glad for it, because it almost gave me an excuse to stay with her a few more days.

"So, you know you do have a place here. You are my flera's sister, after all."

"And I received a message from the Elfin council, your teacher is willing to take you back." Astrid commented.

"And Lord Gael has asked me to stay on to be one of his main healers…" I replied a sad smile on my face.

"Ingrid…"

"I'm fine Astrid, it's just that I would feel a little empty going with them...sadness mostly."

"Because of Anwil?"

Anwil had left a few days after he recovered from his injuries. He had left a note stating that he couldn't stay because he had had a new mission to perform but he would see us again. I hoped that he would be in one piece, he seemed to be lost when he left us.

I looked at sky from the cave that we were in and let the sun hit my face. I looked at the two before me and smiled. I then stood up and hugged my sister and kissed the twin's heads.

"I'll take a little adventure...maybe head to Zodiac and see the healers there. I need time to find my right path."

"We both understand that, but before you go let me give you this." Blagdon replied as he walked over and put something in my palm.

I looked at it to see an amulet with a shape of the dragon carved into it. It was made from a mix of gold and silver, yet it's weight felt lights than that. I looked at the King of Dragons who smiled.

"It's an alloy of gold and silver. It also has magic interwoven into the designs. It will be a plain amulet with different design, but to dragons they will know you are under my protection and will help you in any way they can."

"Thank you." I said with a small smile.

I then walked over to my sister who hugged me tight.

"Before you go, please visit our brothers and uncle, they miss ya and don't forget to write about your adventures."

"I won't, and you make sure you and the twins stay safe."

"We will."

The twins cooed, and I kissed their heads one more time before leaving the room. I had gotten out of the door when I was greeted by Freki and Lord Gael. I shook my head as I smiled at them.

"We decided that a young elf shouldn't travel alone, so being a gentleman I thought to go with you, at least until we're back in Mer."

"Flickron and my father would kill me if I let ye go alone."

"Thank you...both. I wouldn't mind traveling with you for a little while longer." I replied as the three of us left the caves.

As we mounted our horses we stopped and watched as an eagle flew through the sky. I smiled clutching the amulet to my chest and got on my horse. I had a feeling that I was going on a path that would lead me somewhere new, on the true trail of my life not a false one.

"Are your ready Ingrid?" Lord Gael asked.

"Yes, I'm ready to start a new path." I replied as we took our horses reins and left on a new adventure.